The *Pieces* of Summer

A Lancaster County Saga

The *Pieces*
of Summer

Wanda *&*
Brunstetter

BARBOUR
PUBLISHING

Print ISBN 978-1-62029-145-0

eBook Editions:
Adobe Digital Edition (.epub) 978-1-62416-080-6
Kindle and MobiPocket Edition (.prc) 978-1-62416-079-0

All scripture quotations are taken from the King James
Version of the Bible.

This book is a work of fiction. Names, characters, places, and
incidents are either products of the author's imagination or
used fictitiously. Any similarity to actual people, organizations,
and/or events is purely coincidental.

Cover design: Kirk DouPonce, DogEared Design
Cover photography: Steve Gardner, PixelWorks Studios

Published by Barbour Publishing, Inc., P.O. Box 719,
Uhrichsville, Ohio 44683, www.barbourbooks.com

*Our mission is to publish and distribute inspirational products
offering exceptional value and biblical encouragement to the masses.*

Member of the
Evangelical Christian
Publishers Association

Printed in the United States of America.

Peace I leave with you, my peace I give unto you:
not as the world giveth, give I unto you.
Let not your heart be troubled, neither let it be afraid.

JOHN 14:27

CHAPTER 1

Philadelphia, Pennsylvania

When Susan returned to work on Monday morning, she was surprised, as well as pleased, to learn that her John Doe patient had woken up from his coma.

"He's still groggy from all the medication," Nurse Pamela told her as they sat at the nurses' station going over the patients' charts. "But at least he's conscious."

"That's really great news. The poor man has been here since January, and here it is April already. I was beginning to wonder if he'd ever wake up."

"We've all been wondering that," Pamela said with a brief nod. "It's always good to see a patient improve, and hopefully this man you call Eddie will recuperate fully."

"Was he able to say anything? Maybe tell you his name or how he got injured?"

Pamela shook her blond head. "He responded with eyeblinks when we questioned him on how he was feeling, but he was unable to talk. Most likely, it's due to the injury his vocal chords sustained."

"Hopefully, there's no permanent damage, and he'll be able to talk once he starts using his voice again. We need to find out who he is so we can notify his family." Susan stepped out from behind the nurses' station. "I'm going to his room right now to check on him."

When Susan entered the patient's room, she was disappointed to see that his eyes were closed. Was he sleeping, or had he fallen back into a coma?

She took his blood pressure and checked

the rest of his vitals. Since there was no cause for alarm, she seated herself in the chair beside his bed. "Are you awake, Eddie? I heard that you opened your eyes on Saturday."

Susan watched closely, but there was no response. Not even a flutter of his eyelids.

Susan placed her hand on his shoulder. "Heavenly Father, I believe You want this young man to be well, so please continue to touch and heal his body."

Bird-in-Hand, Pennsylvania

Meredith pushed her chair away from the sewing machine and stood. She'd received an order for several more head coverings and had been working on them all morning, so she really needed a break. Her eyes were tired, and her body ached from sitting so long. She felt like she could use a change of scenery and a breath of fresh air.

"Think I'll go outside and check the

mailbox," Meredith called down the stairs to Alma, who was in the basement, washing clothes.

There was no reply. Meredith figured Alma probably had her hearing aids turned off again. Either that or she couldn't hear because of the noise coming from the gas-powered washing machine.

Meredith knew it wouldn't take her long to walk to the end of the driveway to get the mail, so she slipped out the back door, figuring Alma probably wouldn't even know she was gone. A little exercise and some fresh air would be good for her. Being outside always seemed to help, both physically and mentally.

As Meredith approached Fritz's dog run where he was sleeping near the gate, he awoke and started barking and jumping at the fence. "I know, pup," she said, unlatching the gate. "You want to take a walk with me, don't ya, boy?"

Woof! Woof! Fritz licked Meredith's hand and wagged his stubby tail as he romped in circles around her with his lips parted, as though he was grinning.

"Come on then, let's go get the mail!" Meredith clapped her hands and watched as Fritz ran ahead of her. *That dog sure is* schmaert. *He always seems to know just what I'm saying to him.*

Meredith had just reached the mailbox when Sheriff Tyler's car pulled in. As soon as he stepped out of the vehicle, Fritz greeted him with a *yip*, and pranced up beside him.

The sheriff chuckled and bent down to pet Fritz's head. "You're always glad to see me, aren't ya, boy?"

Fritz responded with a wag of his tail.

"Are you getting along okay?" Sheriff Tyler asked, looking back at Meredith.

She nodded.

"You're not staying here alone, I hope."

"Oh, no. Alma Beechy's going to be with me all week while my sister Laurie takes a little holiday to Sarasota, Florida, with her friend Barbara, who's celebrating her birthday this week. They're renting a small house in the village of Pinecraft, where many Amish go for vacation."

"I see. Well, I'm glad you're not alone,

because over the weekend we've had some break-ins in the area, which is part of the reason I stopped by. Besides checking to see how you're doing, I wanted to warn you about these incidents and suggest that you keep your doors locked, even when you're at home. Just to be on the safe side," he quickly added.

Meredith, already feeling a bit apprehensive, shivered and said, "I hadn't heard anything about this before. Have many homes been affected?"

"Just a few, and so far they've all been homes owned by Englishers, but I'm warning everyone in the area, just in case."

"Do you think it's only one person doing these things, or could there be more?" Meredith wasn't sure she wanted to know the answer to that question, but she had to ask. Just the thought of a stranger breaking into her home, let alone several, was frightening enough.

"Wish I could tell you the answer to that," the sheriff replied. "Some of the victims have had more things stolen than others, and it looks like the thieves are after anything that's valuable and could be sold."

Meredith gulped. "It's hard to hear about things like that going on in other places, but you never think it could happen in your own neighborhood. Thanks for letting me know. I appreciate you stopping by."

"Be sure and call my office if you hear or see anything suspicious," he said before getting back in his car and rolling down his window. "It might be a good idea to keep the number for my office in your phone shack. Oh, and please pass the word along to others you may talk to, because I might not be able to get around to everyone today."

"I will, and thank you again, Sheriff Tyler." Meredith waved as he pulled his vehicle back onto the road. Then she quickly took out the mail and headed back to the house. She could see that Fritz was already waiting for her by the back door.

Meredith was glad Alma would be staying with her all week, because knowing there had been some robberies in the area, she'd be even more nervous if she were here all alone.

Her mind was already at work, thinking of ways to make it safer around her home. She was in the habit of locking her doors, especially since Luke had passed away. But even though the weather was getting nicer, Meredith decided that from now on, until the thief had been caught, the pup would be staying in the house with her more, and definitely during the night. She figured Fritz was the best burglar alarm she could possibly have.

Meredith had just stepped onto the porch when a horse and buggy came up the driveway. She turned to look as Fritz barked. Recognizing the horse as Socks, she knew her guest must be Jonah.

"*Wie geht's?*" Jonah asked when he joined her on the porch.

"I'm doing all right," she replied with a smile. "If you came to see Laurie, she's not here. In fact, she'll be gone all week."

Jonah gave his left earlobe a tug. "I'm not here to see Laurie. Came to find out how you're doing, and to give you this." He held out a paper sack. "Happy belated birthday."

Meredith's face heated. "How'd you know I had a birthday?" she asked, feeling a bit hesitant to take the sack.

Fritz sat expectantly looking up at Jonah, probably hoping there was something in the sack for him, because whenever Jonah stopped by he usually had a treat for the dog.

"Back when we were teenagers you mentioned your birthday in one of your letters." He took a step closer, still holding out the sack. "I would have brought this by on your birthday, but things were busy at the buggy shop all day, and I figured you'd be celebrating with your family that evening, so I didn't think it'd be right to come by and interrupt."

Not wishing to be impolite, Meredith took the paper sack, reached inside, and removed several dahlia tubers. "I'm sure these will look nice in my garden when they bloom in the fall," she said. "*Danki*, Jonah."

"Today's my day off, so I have time to plant them for you right now. That is, if you want me to," Jonah said with a wide smile.

Meredith grinned, too, noticing that Fritz

had lost interest and run into the yard to chase after a squirrel.

"I appreciate the offer, but I can put them in the ground myself," she said, bringing her gaze back to Jonah.

Jonah's smile disappeared. "Okay, if that's what you'd prefer." He leaned on the porch railing, as though needing it for support. "Umm. . . Is there something else you'd like me to do?"

She shook her head. "I can't think of anything right now, but I do appreciate your willingness to help."

Fritz leaped back onto the porch and pawed at Jonah's pant leg. Jonah's smile returned as he bent to pet the dog. "You sure like attention, don't ya, boy? Sorry I forgot to bring you a treat, but I'll remember the next time I come over."

Fritz responded with a wag of his tail.

"My folks' dog, Herbie, is the same way," Jonah said, looking at Meredith. "He just can't seem to get enough attention."

"I guess most pets are like that."

Just then, Alma, carrying a wicker basket full of laundry, came around the side of house where the outside basement entrance was.

"Here, let me help you with that," Jonah said, extending his hands.

Alma smiled appreciatively. "Danki, Jonah, that's real nice of you. Would you mind carrying it over to the clothesline for me?"

"Not at all." Jonah took the basket and headed across the yard.

Alma turned to Meredith and smiled. "Jonah is one of the nicest young men I've ever met."

"That's what Laurie says, too," Meredith said. "To tell you the truth, I think she might have a crush on Jonah."

Alma's eyes widened. "You really think so?"

"*Jah*. Haven't you seen the way she acts when he's around—all smiles and full of so many questions?"

"I hadn't really noticed." Alma rubbed her chin thoughtfully. "But I have seen the way Jonah lights up whenever he looks at you."

Meredith's face heated again, and she knew without question that her cheeks must be bright pink. If Jonah was interested in her, she wasn't sure what to do about it. Luke had only been gone a few months, and it was too soon for her to even be thinking about a relationship with another man. Surely Jonah must realize that, too. Maybe he had no desire to be anything more to her than a good friend. Maybe Alma was just imagining things.

And what about Laurie? Meredith thought. *If she is interested in Jonah, which I'm quite sure she is, she'd be hurt if she thought Jonah was after me.*

"Please don't say anything to anyone about your suspicions," Meredith said to Alma.

Alma squeezed Meredith's arm gently. "I won't say a thing. But mark my words: eventually that man's gonna ask you to marry him."

Philadelphia

Where am I? the man wondered as he opened his eyes. He was conscious of voices, but none of them sounded familiar. Were they discussing him? If so, why? Was he sick or injured? There must be something terribly wrong, because it hurt when he breathed, and he couldn't talk.

He tried to raise his head, but he couldn't do that, either. Why did he feel so strange?

"It's okay, Eddie. Just lie still and relax." A young woman with dark hair and dark eyes stood a short distance away, smiling down at him.

Why did she call me, Eddie? Where am I? he silently screamed, but he couldn't form the words.

"You're in the hospital," the woman said, as though sensing what he wanted to know.

How many days have I been here? How bad am I hurt? Was I in an accident or something? So many questions swam around in his brain it made his head hurt even more trying to think things through. All he wanted to do was sleep and escape the pain.

"It's okay," the woman said, placing her hand on his arm. "You've been through a lot. What you need more than anything is lots of rest. When your throat heals sufficiently and you can talk, we hope you'll be able to tell us who you are and what happened to you."

I've been through a lot? What does she mean? I wish I knew what happened to me, the man thought as he closed his eyes and succumbed to sleep.

Bird-in-Hand

That evening as Meredith lay sleeping, she was awakened by a strange noise. Fritz must have heard it, too, for he began to growl.

Thinking maybe Alma had gotten out of bed and bumped into something in the guest room, Meredith grabbed the flashlight on her nightstand and got up. After slipping into her robe, she tiptoed across the hall to Alma's room.

The elderly woman lay curled on her side, snoring softly. Meredith noticed that Alma's hearing aids were lying on the dresser, which explained why the strange noise hadn't awakened her.

With Fritz still growling and walking at her side, Meredith stepped back into the hall and listened. There it was again—a noisy clatter.

Slowly, Meredith made her way down the stairs, with Fritz plodding right beside her, ears perked and head cocked, as though ready for action.

When Meredith's feet touched the bottom step, she heard the noise again—this time much louder. She was sure it was coming from the basement.

A sense of panic welled in her chest. There was definitely someone down there. What if whoever had been breaking into people's houses had somehow gotten into her cellar? *But how could that be?* she reasoned. *I was careful to keep all the doors locked today.*

Then a thought popped into Meredith's head. When Alma had done the laundry this morning, maybe she'd forgotten to lock the outside basement door. Meredith wished Luke was with her right now, because she was really scared. She was sure Luke would have known what to do. Alma was no help, either, since she was sleeping, and Meredith hated to wake her. Besides, if there was someone in the basement, what could two helpless women—one heavy with child, and one quite elderly—do to prevent a robbery?

One thing Meredith knew for sure—she wasn't going to the basement to check on that noise! Who knew what kind of person could be down there? From the sound of things, whoever it was must be rummaging through everything. In her basement were several metal storage cabinets, where Luke had kept a few extra tools that he'd used occasionally around the house. There were also some paint cans, and shelves with household supplies, such as paper towels, napkins, and garbage bags, but nothing Meredith could think of that would be of interest to a robber to steal—unless, of course, he was after the tools.

She quickly grabbed a kitchen chair and propped it against the door, making sure the top of it was securely under the doorknob. Then, grabbing her jacket, and telling Fritz to come with her, she hurried out the back door. She needed to get to the phone shack right away and call the sheriff. She just hoped that chair would keep the intruder from entering the main part of the house, because poor Alma was still upstairs by herself.

CHAPTER 2

$\mathcal{M}$eredith's hand shook as she reached for the phone to dial the sheriff's number. Thankfully, she'd done as Sheriff Tyler suggested and tacked the number for his office to the wall inside the shack. She assumed he wouldn't be in his office at this hour, but surely someone would be there to answer the phone. Or maybe it would be better just to call 911, because she was sure whomever she talked to would send help.

Woof! Woof! Woof! Fritz barked frantically

from outside the phone shack, and Meredith cringed. *Maybe I should have left him in the house to protect Alma. But if I'd done that, his barking might have woken Alma, and she wouldn't have understood what was going on.*

Meredith felt so rattled, she could barely think straight, much less make a phone call. *If Luke was here with me right now, I wouldn't feel so afraid and confused.*

With trembling fingers, Meredith made the 911 phone call. After she'd told the dispatcher there was an intruder in her basement, she was warned not to go back in the house but to wait in the phone shack for help to arrive.

Meredith didn't want to go back to the house, but the thought of leaving Alma there all alone made her nervous.

Remain calm, a voice in her head seemed to say. *Remain calm and stay put like you were told to do.*

She thought about the verse of scripture she'd read the other day: *"Peace I leave with you, my peace I give unto you: not as the world giveth, give I unto you. Let not your heart be troubled, neither let it be afraid" John 14:27.*

Feeling a bit more relaxed, Meredith paused to offer a prayer. "Heavenly Father, please keep Alma and me safe, and send us some help real soon."

Meredith opened the door and let Fritz into the phone shack with her. It should keep him from barking and help her remain calmer, too. She didn't want Fritz's yapping to alert whoever was in the basement any more than it might already have.

It seemed like an eternity before she saw the sheriff's car pull into the yard. She was glad it was him and not some other officer she didn't know very well.

"We were on patrol and received word that you'd called about an intruder," Sheriff Tyler said when he and his deputy, Earl Graves, got out of the car.

Meredith nodded, relieved that help was finally there. "The intruder's in the basement. I wedged a chair in front of the basement door, so hopefully he won't get into the main part of the house."

The sheriff gave her a nod. "Good thinking.

Did you get a look at him, or did he say anything to you?"

"No, but I know someone's in the basement because of all the noise I heard coming from down there. It sounded like they were rummaging through everything, although I don't know why, because there's nothing really valuable down there."

"Well, you'd better stay out here and let us handle the situation." Sheriff Tyler looked at his deputy. "Let's go, Earl."

With the door of the phone shack partially open, Meredith watched as the two men entered her house. "*Ach*, my. . .I hope Alma's all right."

Meredith prayed as she waited, but when she heard someone scream, she couldn't wait any longer. She had to know if Alma was okay.

With Fritz on her heels, Meredith, cradling her stomach with her hands, ran as fast as she could to the house. She'd just entered through the back door, and lit a gas lantern, when she heard the sheriff holler, "Get that feisty fellow, Earl! See if you can trap him in one of those empty boxes."

Meredith's forehead wrinkled. Who in the world was in her basement? Only a child could fit in a box. Was it possible that one of her neighbors' children had gotten into her basement? But it was the middle of the night, so that made no sense.

Meredith crept closer to the basement door, keeping a firm grip on Fritz's collar, but jumped back when she heard a loud crash. She was glad she hadn't gone into the basement when she'd first heard the noise. Whoever was down there must be putting up a fight.

"You okay, Sheriff?" Earl yelled.

"Yeah. Just tripped over some boxes and fell on the floor. Sure wish there was a light I could turn on down here. Can't see much with just our flashlights."

"Did ya trap him, Sheriff?"

"Nope. He got away from me again. Oops. . .there he is now. . . Open the basement door and we'll see if we can chase him out."

Meredith wasn't sure whether the sheriff was referring to the outside basement door or the one that led to the kitchen. But the next thing she knew, Earl let out a yelp, and the inside basement door swung open. A few seconds later, a fat little raccoon darted into the kitchen, with Earl right behind it.

"What are you doin' in here?" he shouted, nearly bumping into Meredith. "Thought the sheriff told ya to wait outside."

Meredith answered the deputy's question, but her voice was drowned out when Fritz started yapping and chasing after the raccoon. Round and round the room they went, bumping into the table, the cupboards, and even the stove. The animal with the masklike eyes skirted past Fritz and jumped on the countertop, knocking over a canister of flour. Talk about Fritz being in the wrong place at the wrong time! The flour not only spilled onto the countertop but cascaded down onto the dog's head and body, just as he ran under the falling powdery white stuff.

Yip! Yip! Yip! Fritz now looked more like a white Dalmatian than the German shorthaired pointer he truly was, with only a few spots of brown color showing from his coat.

Fritz sneezed, sending puffs of flour from

his nostrils, and tried to gain traction on the slippery white mess as he pursued the bandit-looking creature with determination. Sheriff Tyler and Deputy Earl were hot on the chase, slipping and sliding where Fritz had just been, while Meredith stood back, watching the whole thing as she struggled not to laugh. It was really quite a comical scene, and she felt relief, knowing the intruder was just an animal and not a robber after all.

Finally, with Fritz nipping at its bushy ringed tail, the varmint darted out the open back door and into the yard.

"Whew! That's a relief," Sheriff Tyler said, quickly shutting the door. "Don't know how that critter got in your basement, but he sure gave us a merry chase."

"What's going on in here?" Alma asked, yawning as she stepped into the room. "I woke up to use the bathroom, and as soon as I put my hearing aids in, I heard a ruckus down here in the kitchen."

Seeing Alma look around in obvious disbelief at the mess in the kitchen, Meredith quickly explained what had happened. Flour dust was still in the air, but it slowly settled, leaving a film on all the surfaces. Everyone burst out laughing when Deputy Earl removed his glasses that were also coated with flour particles.

When their laughter subsided, the sheriff smiled and said, "When I responded to this call I knew it couldn't have been the fellows who'd done the robberies in the area, because they were caught a few hours after I stopped by your place to warn you about them. I was a bit concerned, however, thinking we might have another thief in the area."

"In a way, there was." Deputy Earl motioned to the floor, where a hunk of carrot lay. "I think that critter was all set to raid the root vegetables you've been storin' in your cellar," he said, looking at Meredith.

Alma slipped her arm gently around Meredith's waist. "The next time Jonah drops by, I'll ask him to check for any places in the basement where an animal might get in and fix it so that nothing like this happens again."

Meredith shook her head. "Let's not bother Jonah with that. I can ask my *daed* or Dorine's husband, Seth, to do it. Right now," she said, looking around at the mess, "I have a kitchen to clean up and a disgruntled dog to bathe."

Darby, Pennsylvania

"I sure like this straw hat you got for me at the farmers' market," Susan's grandfather said as the two of them worked together in the garden early Tuesday morning. "It helps to keep the sun out of my eyes."

"I'm glad you're pleased with it, Grandpa." Susan stabbed her shovel into the ground and pulled up another clump of weeds. It felt good to be outdoors in the fresh spring air, with her hands in the dirt. Gardening was kind of a hobby for her, and she found a sense of satisfaction in it. Grandpa obviously felt the same way, because ever since the weather had turned nice, he'd been spending several hours each day outside in the yard. Susan didn't have the luxury of gardening that often, though. Most of the time when she got home from the hospital, she was either too tired to work in the yard or it was late and already dark. Today, her shift wouldn't begin until noon, so she'd taken advantage of the early morning hours to help Grandpa get some weeding done.

"Eww. . .look at this." Susan wrinkled her nose as she watched a lengthy, plump earthworm wiggling from the dirt, still clinging to the bottom of the weed in her gloved hand.

"Now that's a good one." Grandpa bobbed his head. "If I had plans to go fishing soon, I'd suggest puttin' the wiggler in my bait box. But for now, you can just throw him in one of your grandma's flower beds. It'll be good for the soil."

Susan did as Grandpa suggested. "Oops! I missed the flower bed," she said, watching as the worm landed in the grass.

"Don't worry about it," Grandpa said. "The ground's damp over there, and I'm sure it'll worm its way under the grass and into the dirt."

Susan was just getting ready to pull another

weed when she noticed movement out of the corner of her eye. She pointed in the direction where Grandpa was already looking, watching a robin gobble up the worm she'd just tossed onto the grass.

"See what fun your sister is missing?" Grandpa chuckled as Susan made a face. "I tried to talk Anne into joining us out here," he said, "but she turned me down flat. Guess she'd rather put on her jogging clothes and run all over the neighborhood, working up a sweat, than dig in the dirt with us."

Susan laughed and wiped the perspiration from her forehead. "And what do you think we're doing out here, if not sweating?"

He grinned and yanked up another weed. "This is different. At least when we work up a sweat, we have somethin' to show for our troubles. The only thing Anne has to show for all that jogging she does every day is a skinny body, without an ounce of flab."

"Well, you know my sister. . . She does like to keep fit and trim, which I'm sure helps her as a physical therapist."

Grandpa grunted. "She could get fit and trim pullin' weeds, I'll bet."

"Not everyone likes gardening the way we do," Susan reminded him. "Grandma doesn't like it that much, and it doesn't seem to bother you any."

"Well, she might not like to pull weeds, but she does cook all the produce we grow." Grandpa jiggled his eyebrows playfully. "Yes indeed, my wife's a mighty good cook."

Susan smiled. "I can't argue with that."

They worked in silence for a while, until Grandpa set his shovel aside and said, "Think we got most of the weeds out now, don't you?"

"Yes, but a few days from now, there will probably be more." Susan motioned to the picnic table under the leafy maple tree in the corner of the yard. "Should we sit awhile and visit before it's time for me to get ready for work?" she asked.

"Sounds good to me."

After they'd both taken a seat on the picnic bench, Susan turned to Grandpa and said, "When I got home from the hospital last night, you and Grandma were already in bed, so I didn't get the chance to tell you that Eddie finally woke up."

Grandpa's thick eyebrows lifted high on his forehead. "That John Doe patient of yours?"

She nodded. "I guess he came out of the coma on Saturday while Anne and I were in Lancaster County. One of the nurses told me about it when I got to work yesterday."

"That's good news, Susan. Did you get to talk to the young man?"

She shook her head. "Unfortunately, he slept through most of my shift, and due to the injury to his vocal cords, even when he was awake, he was unable to talk. I'm hoping it won't be long before he can communicate. I'm really anxious to find out who he is and how he got injured."

CHAPTER 3

Bird-in-Hand

$\mathcal{D}$id you have a nice time in Florida?" Meredith asked when Laurie showed up at her house the following Monday morning.

Laurie nodded enthusiastically, her face fairly glowing. "Oh, jah. It was a lot of fun spending time on the beach. No wonder you stayed in Sarasota a whole summer when you were eighteen. I think I could live there, too."

"You're nice and brown, so it looks like you got plenty of sun," Meredith said, making no comment about the time she'd spent in Florida. Sometimes she wished she could return to those carefree teenage days, when all she had to worry about was being courteous to the customers at the restaurant where she'd worked and enjoying her free time at the beach.

"I sure did get some sun." Laurie held out her arms. "With my fair skin, I had to be careful not to burn, so I used plenty of sunscreen. It must have helped, because I look more tan than burned."

"What else did you do besides go to the beach?" Meredith asked, glancing at her own arms, which were as pale as ever.

"Oh, we. . ." Laurie stopped talking and dropped her gaze to the floor. "So, have you seen Jonah lately?" she asked, abruptly changing the subject.

"He's dropped by a few times. Why do you ask?"

"Oh, just curious, is all."

"Do you like him?" Meredith questioned, curious at how quickly Laurie had changed the subject.

"Who?" Laurie dropped into a seat on the sofa.

"Jonah."

"Of course I do." Laurie smiled. "He's a very nice man."

Meredith hesitated a minute, wondering how best to express her thoughts. "I know you are interested in him, but I don't think it's good for you to be so obvious about it," she said, taking a seat beside her sister.

Laurie's forehead wrinkled. "What are you talking about, Meredith? I've never said I was interested in Jonah."

"Maybe not in so many words, but whenever he comes around, you smile at him and seem to be hanging on his every word."

Laurie's cheeks flamed. "I'm not the least bit interested in Jonah. I just know he's a good friend of yours, and since he might end up to be my brother-in-law someday, I thought I should be nice to him."

Meredith's mouth dropped open. "Wh— where did you come up with that idea?"

"I've seen the way he looks at you, Meredith.

It's obvious that he's smitten."

"You can tell that just by how he looks at me?"

Laurie shrugged. "That's only part of it. I don't think Jonah would come over here so often, wanting to help out, if he wasn't interested in you."

Meredith shook her head. "That's ridiculous! Jonah's just a friend, and he knows I'm still mourning Luke's death."

"That doesn't mean he's not interested in having a relationship with you whenever you're ready."

Meredith stared straight ahead. "I don't think I'll ever be ready for that. I love Luke, and I always will."

Laurie placed her hand on Meredith's arm. "Of course you will, but it doesn't mean you can never love another man. Luke wouldn't want you to grieve for him forever. He'd want you to be happy and find love again."

"How do you know what Luke would want?" The pitch of Meredith's voice raised a notch. "You can't speak for him."

"I realize that," Laurie said, "but I know

Luke loved you very much, and I'm sure he would want you to move on with your life and, most of all, be happy again."

"That's easy for you to say." Meredith instinctively looked around the living room at all the things that reminded her of Luke. "You don't understand what it's like for me."

"No, I don't, but I do know how it feels to be in love." Laurie clamped her hand over her mouth. "I—I. . .What I meant to say was. . ."

"You said a few minutes ago that you're not interested in Jonah, so if not him, then who?" Meredith questioned, bringing her focus back on her sister.

"I—I'd rather not say," Laurie mumbled.

"If you've come to care about someone, then why not just admit it? What have you got to hide?"

"Do you promise not to tell?"

"Tell who? Mom and Dad?"

Laurie nodded. "If they knew who I've been seeing secretly, they'd be *umgerennt*."

"Why would they be upset? Who is it, Laurie? Who have you been seeing that Mom and Dad wouldn't approve of?"

"Kevin Byler," Laurie said in a near whisper.

"But Kevin's not Amish, Laurie. You know what that would mean if you married him?"

"It would mean I wouldn't join the Amish church like I'd planned to do this fall. But at least I'd be going to Kevin's Mennonite church, and they preach God's Word there, too."

Meredith sighed. She knew how much their folks, and especially Mom, were looking forward to seeing Laurie baptized into the Amish faith. She also knew, or at least hoped, that their folks would show some understanding if Laurie and Kevin decided to get married.

Meredith gave her sister a hug. "I won't tell Mom and Dad that you've been seeing Kevin, but if you two are getting serious, then you need to tell them yourself, and soon, before they hear about it from someone else. News travels fast in our community, and if anyone's seen you and Kevin together, there is bound to be talk."

Tears welled in Laurie's eyes. "I know you're right. Kevin has a stand at the farmers' market, too, and we've sometimes taken our lunches together, but we've always gone somewhere outside the market, where Dad and the others who work there couldn't see."

Meredith looked her sister straight in the eyes. "Was Kevin with you in Florida last week?"

Laurie sniffed deeply as she gave a slow nod. "We weren't alone, though. Three other couples were with us. Oh, and the girls stayed together in one of the places we rented, and the guys stayed in another," she quickly added.

Meredith couldn't believe her sister had been so deceitful, but then she didn't think it was her place to judge Laurie. "From one sister to another, I'd like to give you some advice," she said, giving Laurie's shoulder a gentle squeeze.

"What's that?"

"Go to Mom and Dad as soon as possible and tell them the way you feel about Kevin. They may not like it at first, but at least this secret won't be between you anymore, and you'll feel better once you've apologized and stopped sneaking around. It never does anyone any good to be deceitful. Besides, you know it

WANDA E. BRUNSTETTER

would hurt Mom and Dad deeply if they heard about this from anyone other than you."

"I know," Laurie said tearfully. "I feel better already, just having told you." She leaned forward and gave Meredith a hug.

❧

Jonah whistled as he guided his horse and buggy down the road toward Meredith's house. He was in good spirits this morning—partly because it was such a beautiful spring day, but mostly because his horse was behaving so well. Jonah had figured when he'd first bought Socks from Meredith that it was just a matter of time before the frisky animal got to know and trust him, and he'd been right. Each time he took the gelding out on the road, things had gone better than the time before. Now Socks obeyed all of Jonah's commands and didn't try to run when he wasn't supposed to. Apparently all the horse needed was time to adjust to his original owner being gone. And Jonah's persistence in trying to win the horse over had no doubt played a role in the animal's improved behavior, too.

When Jonah arrived at Meredith's, he was surprised to see her out working in the garden. After nearly losing the baby a few months ago, he was under the impression that she would need to take it easy right up until the baby was born.

Once Jonah had Socks secured at the hitching rail, he hurried across the yard to the garden, where Meredith was pulling up weeds.

"Should you be doing that?" he asked after he'd said hello. "It might be a little too strenuous for you."

Her lips pursed as she stared up at him, the sun making the sides of her strawberry-blond tresses look like golden threads. It was all Jonah could do to keep from reaching under her head covering and touching her hair.

"I'm not overdoing," Meredith was quick to say. "The exercise is good for me, and if I don't get these weeds pulled, I won't have a garden."

"*Ungraut rope aus em gaarde is ken gschpass,*" Jonah said, kneeling on the grass beside her.

Her face relaxed a bit. "I guess you're right.

Weeding a garden would be more fun if I wasn't doing it alone. Laurie's back from Florida now, and she was going to help me, but she's busy washing clothes at the moment."

"It's not a problem, because I'm here now, and I'm more than willing to help." Jonah dug his fingers into the dirt and snatched up a weed.

Meredith wrinkled her nose. "Don't you want a shovel or a spade to do that? It's much easier on your fingers and nails."

Jonah chuckled. "Working on buggies the way I do with my daed is harder on my hands than pullin' weeds. But if you have another hand shovel I can use, that might make it easier to dig out the roots of these nasty ungraut."

Meredith motioned to the small shed near the barn. "You'll find several sizes of shovels in there."

"Great. I'll go get one." Jonah rose and strode across the yard to the shed.

"My sister and Alma think you're really a nice man," Meredith said when he returned with a small shovel and started pulling weeds.

"What about you, Meredith? Do you think

I'm a nice man, too?" he asked, glancing over at her.

Meredith's cheeks warmed. "Of course I do. I've always thought you were nice. You've been more than helpful to me since Luke died, and I appreciate it very much."

Jonah smiled. "Guess it's just in my nature to be that way. Least that's how it's been ever since a kid I didn't even know cared enough to save me from drowning when I was just a boy. Since that time, I've had a new appreciation for life, and whenever I see someone who has a need, I try to help them as much as I can."

Meredith returned his smile. "That's a good way to be, because it's what the Bible teaches us to do."

He nodded as he shook the dirt loose from the clump of weeds he'd just pulled out from between some pea plants. "Jah, that's so true."

They worked for a while in companionable silence, until the *clip-clop* of horse's hooves interrupted their quiet. Meredith shielded her eyes from the glare of the sun, gazing across the yard to see whose buggy it was.

A few seconds later, Luke's mother, Sadie, stepped down from the buggy and secured her horse at the hitching rail. A frown creased her brow as she approached the garden. Was she upset about something? Had she come with bad news?

"Wie geht's?" Meredith asked.

"I'm fine," Sadie said curtly. "I just came by to see how you're doing." She glanced at Jonah, frowned slightly, and then quickly looked away.

Meredith thought Sadie's behavior was a bit strange; she was usually quite warm and friendly.

"I'm doing okay," Meredith said. "Jonah stopped by awhile ago, and he's helping me pull some weeds."

"I can certainly see that." Sadie motioned to her buggy. "I brought you some of Luke's baby clothes, thinking you could use them when the *boppli* gets here. Should I take the box inside?"

"I'll get it for you," Jonah offered, rising to his feet. Before Sadie could respond, he'd sprinted to her buggy. While Jonah hauled the box to the house, Meredith and Sadie visited.

"Isn't Alma here with you today?" Sadie questioned.

"No, Laurie's here today. She's in the basement, washing clothes."

As if on cue, Laurie came around the house, carrying a basket full of laundry. She smiled at Sadie as she walked by. "It's nice to see you."

Sadie smiled in return. "Same here."

"Do you need my help hanging the laundry?" Meredith asked.

"No, that's okay, I can manage. Just enjoy your time visiting with Sadie." Laurie hurried away and began clipping the clothes to the line.

When Jonah came out of the house, Sadie turned to Meredith and said, "Should we go inside and look through the box of baby things now?"

"That'd be fine," Meredith replied, "but I may not be able to use all of Luke's baby clothes."

Sadie's eyebrows furrowed. "Why not?"

Meredith placed her hands against her bulging stomach. "I don't know yet if the boppli's a *bu* or a *maedel*."

Sadie nodded. "That's true, but many of the sleepers and blankets are in neutral colors, so

49

you should be able to use those for either a boy or a girl."

"I'll pull the rest of these weeds while you two go look at the clothes," Jonah called as Meredith and Sadie headed toward the house.

Meredith stopped walking and turned to face him. "There isn't too much left to do, and I appreciate all the help you've already given me, so you really don't have to finish the job. I can do it later."

Jonah shook his head with a determined expression. "There's no need for that. It'll only take me a short time, and then I'll be on my way home."

"Danki, Jonah." Meredith smiled; then she followed her mother-in-law into the house.

When they entered the living room, Sadie turned to Meredith with a deep frown wrinkling her forehead. "How often has Jonah been coming around here? He seems awfully familiar with you."

Meredith stiffened. "What are you getting at, Sadie?"

"I just don't think it's right for him to be

here—especially when you're a young widow, expecting a boppli."

Meredith sighed deeply. "Jonah is just a good friend, and all he wants to do is help out. I'm sorry if you don't think he should be here, but I won't hurt his feelings by telling him not to come over anymore."

Sadie opened her mouth, but then she snapped it closed and folded her arms.

"Let's look at Luke's baby clothes now," Meredith suggested. "I appreciate you bringing them over."

❦

When Sadie arrived home later that morning, she found her husband, Elam, sitting on the front porch with a glass of lemonade.

"How was your visit with Meredith?" he asked, taking a sip of the refreshing drink. "Was she glad to get the baby clothes?"

"I think so," Sadie replied, "but that buggy-maker's son, Jonah, was there."

Elam quirked an eyebrow. "Oh?"

"Jah, and I don't think it's right that he's been hanging around there so much. I'm afraid he's trying to take Luke's place, and it's way too soon for Meredith to be seeing another man." She placed her hand on Elam's shoulder. "I think you should do something about it, and the sooner the better."

"What do you want me to do, Sadie?" Elam asked, shrugging his shoulders. "Am I supposed to barge into the buggy shop and demand that Jonah stay away from Meredith?"

"That might not be a bad idea," she said with a nod.

Elam looked at her and frowned as he slowly shook his head. "If Jonah and Meredith are meant to be together, there's nothing either one of us can do about it."

Sadie's lips compressed while she tapped her foot. "We'll just have to see about that."

CHAPTER 4

As the cooler days of spring turned into warmer days of summer, Meredith grew weary of everyone doing things for her. It was the middle of June, and her stomach had grown much bigger. She missed the physical work she could no longer do because she was so top-heavy. This morning, she felt almost worthless, wishing she could do more than sit and sew.

She moved from the kitchen to stand in

front of the screen door and drew in a deep breath. The sweet smelling scent of the lilacs blooming along the property line wafted up to her nose. The butterflies obviously liked them, too, she noticed, as they glided from one bloom to the next.

Meredith smiled, watching the birds in her yard flitting from the trees to the feeders she kept filled for her enjoyment as much as providing for the birds. Jonah had come by a few weeks ago and repaired a couple of the feeders that had been damaged during a strong wind they'd had in the middle of May.

Jonah had been so kind to her and helped out in many ways. Mom had her hands full, taking care of the children still living at home. Dad kept busy with his stands at the markets, not to mention the chores he had to do at home, so he didn't have much free time at all. Luke's folks helped out sometimes, too, but they were getting up in their years, and Meredith didn't feel right about asking either of them to do a lot—especially with some of the heavier things that needed to be done. So with Jonah helping Meredith, she didn't have to call on anyone else too often.

Meredith enjoyed Jonah coming by; he was easy to talk to. She felt more comfortable in his presence than she had at first. He listened and seemed to understand the way she felt about things. At first, she'd been a bit uneasy about him doing things around the place to help out, but that was getting less awkward, especially as she grew in her pregnancy. Jonah had shared some things with her about his twin sister, Jean, and how it had been for her when she'd lost her first husband. He had tried to help her as much as possible and had been there to listen and offer support whenever she'd needed a shoulder to cry on. It seemed obvious to Meredith that Jonah was not only a good brother but also a friend she could count on.

Meredith's one concern, which was never far from her thoughts, was her financial situation. Her home-based business of making head coverings for Amish women was helping some, but it was hard to stretch her budget every month, even with the money her parents and Luke's folks sometimes insisted that she take. There had also been a charity auction in their community last month, and she'd been given some of the money from that to help with expenses. Every little bit helped, but how long would it last? Others in the community needed help, too, and Meredith wanted to be able to make it on her own.

She was glad Dad hadn't taken on another stand at the Crossroads market, like he'd talked about doing a few months ago. He worked hard enough as it was, and it was difficult for the family to have him gone so much. It was important for a father to spend time with his wife and children, not only for the family's sake but for his own, as well.

Thinking about fathers and their children caused Meredith to choke up. Her precious baby would never know his father. But she would make sure the little one knew all about Luke and what a wonderful husband he had been, and how she'd loved him so much. Meredith tried not to dwell on the past or reflect too much about the future. She didn't even want to think about how she would make it through the days ahead. It was best just to take one day at a time and trust the Lord to meet all of her needs.

Meredith's thoughts shifted to her sister Laurie. She'd been back from Florida for almost two months and still hadn't told their parents about Kevin. Meredith kept reminding Laurie that the longer she put it off, the harder it was going to be, and Laurie kept promising she would say something soon.

What is she waiting for? Meredith wondered. *It will be a lot worse if our folks hear the news from someone else.*

"Why don't we go outside and enjoy the sunshine for a bit?" Alma asked, joining Meredith at the screen door and interrupting her thoughts.

"I really should be at the sewing machine right now," Meredith replied, "but I guess I can do that after we've enjoyed the warmth of the sun for a while."

Philadelphia

As Susan made her rounds in ICU that morning, she felt a keen sense of disappointment. Eddie, her John Doe patient, had been moved to rehab two weeks ago, and she missed seeing him every day. As luck would have it, though, her sister, Anne, had been assigned as Eddie's physical therapist, so she saw him several times a week and always gave Susan a full report on how he was progressing. During supper last night, she'd told Susan that she'd been working with Eddie to regain the strength in his legs. He'd been confined to his bed for so many months, and even though they'd exercised his legs when he was in a coma, he'd been left unable to walk on his own.

Another therapist worked with Eddie vocally. Serious damage to his vocal cords had left him unable to speak for a time, but he was now talking again—although his voice sounded gravelly and hoarse and would probably always

58

be that way. He was also receiving memory-training therapy, but so far Eddie's mind remained a blank.

I think I'll stop by the rehab center when I get off work today, Susan told herself. *I'd like to see for myself how Eddie is doing and let him know that I'm still praying for him.*

Eddie groaned and clicked the button to change the channel on the TV above his bed. One of the nurses had shown him how to work the remote, because he'd had a hard time trying to figure it out. The programs seemed strange to him, too—like he'd never seen them before. *Maybe I didn't have a TV,* he thought. *Or is that just another thing I've forgotten about?*

Susan, the nurse he'd had before they moved him for therapy, had said he'd been found in the bathroom of the bus depot in Philadelphia, wearing nothing but a pair of dirty blue jeans and a holey T-shirt. She'd also told him that he'd been beaten up pretty badly and might have died if he hadn't been found in time.

Eddie. The nurses all call me that, but they say it's not my real name. Who am I, really, and how did I end up in the hospital in such bad condition?

Eddie didn't remember anything at all about his life before waking up in the hospital. It was frustrating to have so many unanswered questions swimming around in his head, as if he'd just been born, knowing nothing at all.

What was I doing in the bus station? Was I traveling somewhere? he wondered. *Who beat me up, and why?* There was so much to figure out, and he didn't know how to piece any of it together. His head hurt when he tried to think. *If I could just remember who I am and what my life was like before coming here. Did I have a job in the city? If so, what did I do for a living? Was I married? Did I have children? Or was I some poor man on the street with no home or family of my own?*

"I'm hungry," Eddie murmured, breaking free from his troubling thoughts. He pushed his call button, but no one responded. He waited awhile and pushed it again. Still no reply.

He frowned. *Guess I'll get up and head down*

to the nurses' station.

Holding on to the side rail, Eddie crawled out of bed. As soon as his feet hit the floor, a wave of dizziness and nausea washed over him. He'd been told that due to the severe head injury he'd sustained, he might have trouble with headaches and wooziness for quite some time. He stood still until his head quit swimming then took a step forward. The room started spinning again, and everything visible whirled into one. The TV blended in with the window, and then the window merged into the picture hanging on the wall. He closed his eyes to try to regain his balance, but his legs felt like rubber. Try as he might, Eddie couldn't walk on his own. Instead, he wobbled and dropped to the floor with a groan.

Bird-in-Hand

I'm glad Elam's visiting his friend Joe today, Sadie thought as she hitched her horse, Daisy, to the buggy. *If he knew I was going over to confront Jonah about seeing Meredith, he'd probably tell me I shouldn't go and that it's none of my business what Jonah does.*

Sadie had wanted to pay a call on Jonah sooner but hadn't had the chance until today. The last week of April, she and Elam had gone to watch their granddaughter Mary Beth's end-of-the-year school program in Gratz. From there they'd made a trip to Wisconsin to see Elam's brother Sam, who had been in the hospital after suffering a stroke. They'd stayed until he was out of the hospital and had returned home only two days ago. After running into Meredith's mother at the grocery store yesterday and hearing that Jonah had continued going over to Meredith's on a regular basis, Sadie decided it was time to pay him a visit.

As Sadie headed down the road with her horse and buggy, she rehearsed what she would say to Jonah. She wouldn't beat around the bush or make light of the situation. She'd get right to the point and tell him in no uncertain words how she felt about things.

When Sadie arrived at the Millers' place,

she stopped at the buggy shop, thinking Jonah would be working there. But then seeing a CLOSED sign in the shop window, she headed straight for the house.

Jonah's mother, Sarah, answered the door. "It's nice to see you, Sadie. Can I help you with something, or did you just drop by for a visit?" she asked.

"I came to see Jonah," Sadie replied stiffly. "I need to speak with him about something."

"Today is Jonah's day off, and he's out in the barn getting his horse ready because he'll be going fishing soon."

"Oh, I see. I'll go out there and speak to him then." Without waiting for Sarah's response, Sadie turned and hurried off toward the barn. She found Jonah about to lead his horse out of the stall.

"I need to speak with you," Sadie said, boldly stepping up to Jonah.

"About what?" he asked with a curious expression.

"I don't think it's right for you to be going over to Meredith's so much. It's only been a little over five months since our son Luke died, and Meredith is still quite vulnerable."

Jonah smiled, although it appeared to be forced. "I assure you, Sadie, Meredith and I are only friends, and actually, I'd be there for anyone who needed my help, not just your daughter-in-law."

"It's good to be helpful, but I think it would be best if you stop seeing Meredith."

Jonah's dark eyebrows pulled together. "Unless Meredith asks me to stop going over to her place, I'll continue to help out."

Sadie frowned deeply. She was not the least bit happy about this, but she didn't say anything more. She knew it wasn't right to hope that Meredith would continue struggling financially, but maybe once the baby came and Meredith was too busy to make head coverings, she'd be willing to move in with Sadie and Elam. She could either sell her house or put it up for rent. If Meredith was living with them, Sadie could help out with the baby, and then she'd be certain that Jonah wouldn't be coming around any longer.

As Jonah meandered along the stream a few miles from his folks' place, he thought about his unexpected visit with Sadie Stoltzfus. He couldn't figure out why she was so upset that he'd been helping Meredith. Couldn't she see that they were just friends?

But I wish it could be more, he admitted to himself. *I wish I could make her my wife. When enough time has passed, I'll tell Meredith how I feel. Maybe she'll come to care for me as much as I do her. I just don't want to rush her, that's all.*

Jonah hadn't told anyone yet, not even Dad, that he loved Meredith. Truth was, he'd fallen in love with her during the time they'd known each other in Florida. Maybe if he hadn't been too timid to tell her back then, she might not have married Luke. Jonah had lived with his mistake for many years. Working hard and keeping busy had helped, but it wasn't like coming home each evening to someone he loved—a wife who shared her life with him.

"Guess there's no point in thinkin' about the past," Jonah mumbled as he stopped beside a tall birch tree that was leaning slightly over the stream. He noticed half the roots from the tree were suspended out over the water, as if reaching for something to cling to. An empty space under the tree had washed out when the water was flowing high.

Jonah pushed against the tree, wondering how long it would stay upright. He figured someday it would end up lying across the stream, creating a natural bridge.

Purdy...purdy...purdy... Jonah looked up and spotted a cardinal sitting on a branch overhead. The music of the bird's singing blended with the gentle sound of green leaves blowing in the warm summer breeze.

Jonah hadn't felt like fishing, after all, so he'd left his pole in the buggy. He had secured Socks to a tree some distance away, and before they headed home, he would bring the horse down to the stream for a good long drink. For now, though, Jonah just wanted to relax and enjoy the beauty of nature. There was no doubt about it—God had created a beautiful world for man to enjoy. It was a shame some people took it for granted and never noticed what was right in front of them, free for their enjoyment.

Wanting to get more comfortable in the warm air, Jonah untucked his shirt to let it hang loosely and rolled up his sleeves. He then took a small box of raisins from his pocket. They tasted good and eased his hunger pangs just a bit.

He threw a few raisins into the water and watched as several minnows came from nowhere to nibble on the morsels as they slowly sank to the bottom of the stream. Jonah tossed in a few more raisins, drawing a huge cluster of the small silvery fish swimming around like they were waiting for another handout.

Leaning against the tree again, Jonah spotted a water snake slithering along and then going under the water's surface where all the fish were gathered.

The tree's roots suddenly gave way, and the tree fell toward the water. Jonah wasn't quick enough to catch himself, and as the tree crashed, his foot became wedged between two of the big roots. He struggled to free it, as the snake swam toward him.

Dear Lord, Jonah prayed, *help me to get out of here fast!*

CHAPTER 5

Philadelphia

When Anne entered the rehab floor and headed for Eddie's room, she whispered a prayer. "Dear Lord, I pray that things will go well with Eddie's therapy today, and help me to be an encouragement to him."

As soon as Anne stepped in her patient's room, she spotted him lying on the floor beside his bed. Relieved to see that he was conscious, although struggling to get up, she quickly squatted down beside him. "Eddie, what happened? Did you try to get out of bed by yourself?"

He nodded, offering her a guilty-looking grin. "I was hungry and thought I could walk down to the nurses' station and ask for something to eat. But the room started spinning, and the next thing I knew, I was flat on the floor."

Anne slipped her arms around his waist and helped him to stand. "You should have punched the call button for help," she said, assisting him back into the bed.

He frowned. "I tried that, but no one came."

"Well, you should have kept trying." She pulled the sheet up and tucked it under his chin. "I'll go see if I can get you something to snack on, and then we need to begin your therapy session."

Eddie's nose wrinkled as he raked his fingers through the ends of his white-blond hair. "What's the point in me learning how to walk on my own when I don't even know who I am? I'm pretty much worthless, and if I ever do get to leave this hospital, I'll probably have to go beg on the streets 'cause I don't even know what I can do to earn a living." He groaned. "Since I have no identification, who'd hire me anyways?"

"Let's take these issues one at a time," Anne said. "I'll be back in a few minutes with some food." She tapped him gently on the arm. "So please stay put."

Anne wasn't sure what else to say. If they knew who Eddie was, and he had a family to take care of him, he could begin life anew. But with no evidence of his identity and not even a glimpse of his lost memory, the poor man was like a ship without any water to stay afloat.

I wonder when Eddie's well enough to leave the hospital, if Grandma and Grandpa might consider taking him in, Anne thought. *They have a big house, with five bedrooms, two of which are vacant, so maybe they'd be charitable enough to let Eddie live there in exchange for him doing some chores around the place. Guess I'll wait to mention that until he's stronger and getting closer to being released.*

As Anne continued down the hall toward the nurses' station, she spotted Susan heading her way.

"I came to visit Eddie," Susan said eagerly. "I wanted to see how he's doing today."

"Well, he was determined enough to get some food that he tried to get out of bed by himself." Anne smiled, despite the seriousness of the situation. "That determination is what's going to help him get well—at least physically. I don't know what it's going to take to bring his memory back."

"Perhaps someone will say or do something that will jog his memory," Susan said with a hopeful expression. "And of course, I'll continue to pray for his full recovery."

Anne nodded. "Same here."

Strasburg, Pennsylvania

Luann King had been out shopping all morning and decided to stop at a sandwich shop for a bite of lunch before going home. Her mother was watching the little ones today, and sixteen-year-old Kendra was there to help out. Laurie and Philip were working at the Bird-in-Hand farmers' market in Bird-in-Hand today, so everyone in the family had something to do.

Luann smiled as she entered the restaurant. It was kind of nice to be out on her own for a while. She didn't get the opportunity to shop by herself that often, much less go out to lunch.

As Luann looked for a place to sit, she spotted a young couple seated at a table with their backs to her. They sat close to each other, with their heads almost touching, as though they were courting. The woman was dressed in Amish clothes, but the young man wore blue jeans and a white T-shirt. Luann figured he could be Amish and going through his time of *rumschpringe*. Or maybe he was English. If that was the case, it would no doubt sadden the young woman's family. Most Amish parents wanted their daughters to be courted by men who wouldn't sway them to leave their Amish way of life.

Luann slipped into a booth across the room, and as she turned to look for a waitress, her mouth dropped open. The young woman at the table across from her was Laurie!

Laurie looked at Luann at about the same time, and her jaw dropped slightly as her eyes widened. "Mom, wh–what are you doing here?" she asked, her face turning red with obvious embarrassment.

Luann rose to her feet and moved over to stand beside Laurie's table. "More to the point, what are *you* doing here? I thought you were supposed to be selling dolls at the farmers' market today."

"Well, I—" Laurie moistened her lips with the tip of her tongue. "I'm on my lunch break right now." She turned to the young man sitting beside her. "Uh, Mom, this is Kevin Byler."

Luann studied Kevin a few seconds then slowly nodded. She hadn't recognized him at first, but now she realized his folks lived just a mile or so down the road from them.

"It's nice to see you, Mrs. King." Kevin smiled and extended his hand.

Luann shook it briefly; then she turned to Laurie and said, "I'm going to the ladies' room. I'd like you to come with me."

Laurie hesitated but finally nodded. She smiled at Kevin and said, "I'll be back soon."

When they entered the restroom, Luann didn't mince any words. "Are you and Kevin seeing each other socially, Laurie?"

"Jah." Laurie dropped her gaze to the floor. "We've been going out for a few months."

"Why didn't you tell your daed and me about this?"

"I—I didn't want to hurt you."

Luann's lips tightened. "Oh, and you don't think I'm hurt right now, finding this out after the fact?"

Laurie placed her hand on Luann's arm. "I'm sorry, Mom. I know I should have said something sooner, but—"

"But you thought it'd be better to sneak around behind our backs?"

Laurie shook her head. "I knew you wouldn't approve, and I was going to tell you, but I just couldn't seem to find the right time, or the right way to say it. I wasn't sure how to explain things to you because I knew you'd be upset."

Luann narrowed her eyes. "Just how serious are you about Kevin?"

Laurie leaned on the counter by the sinks and drew in a quick breath. "I—I love him, Mom. He asked me to marry him, and I said I would."

Luann held her hands stiffly at her sides, fingers clenched until they dug into her palms. "We'll talk more about this at home, after your sisters and brothers have gone to bed."

Bird-in-Hand

Sweat beaded on Jonah's forehead as he struggled to get his foot free from the roots of the tree. Keeping his eye on the water snake, he felt relief when it swam off in the opposite direction, in pursuit of an unsuspecting minnow. The last thing he needed was to be eye-to-eye with a snake!

Jonah's ankle throbbed something awful, and he wondered if it might be broken. One thing he knew for sure: he needed to get his foot unstuck so he could take a look at it and find out how badly he'd been hurt.

Suddenly, an idea popped into his head. If he untied his boot he might be able to slip his foot out, and then he'd be free. It was shocking to Jonah to discover just how deep this particular spot was in the stream, because the water was now well over his chest. Standing on the bank earlier, he'd never imagined the water being more than a few feet deep.

"Talk about bad luck," Jonah mumbled, wondering how he had managed to get into this predicament. He leaned over and reached down until his fingers touched the laces on his boot. The water was very cold, not yet warmed since the return of summer. He could feel, but not see, his boot.

Jonah had never learned to swim that well, and he didn't like to put his face under water, but it would be much easier to see what he was doing if he got closer to the boot. He dreaded it, but realizing he had no other choice, Jonah knew he'd need to go into a sitting position.

Taking in a deep breath, he let his body sink to the water's depth of five or so feet. Being under water brought back memories of the day he'd nearly drowned when he was a boy, and he almost panicked. Pinching his nose shut would have helped, but Jonah needed both hands to untie the wet laces. Feeling the cold water seep into his ears, he just wanted to get this over with.

The water had been clear before the tree fell, but now it was murky with sediment that had been kicked up from the stream's bottom. Under water, peering through the murkiness, Jonah could see parts of the tree root that held his foot securely, but he could barely make out his bootlaces.

Too bad that brave kid's not here to rescue me now, Jonah thought as he fumbled with his laces. He came up once for a breath of air then ducked his head under the muddy-colored water again. This time he was successful in getting his laces untied, and after wiggling his foot around a bit, he was finally able to pull it free from the boot.

Jonah hobbled onto the bank and winced

when he tried to put weight on his bootless left foot. It was either broken or he'd sprained it pretty bad. He stood on his uninjured foot for a moment, shaking his head to one side, trying to get the water out that had clogged his right ear. Finally, after several attempts, he felt the now-warm liquid trickle down over his earlobe.

Using a broken tree limb as a sort of crutch, Jonah hobbled over to the tree where he'd secured his horse. After untying Socks, he climbed into the buggy and took up the reins. Once he got out to the highway, Socks took off like a shot. It was almost as if he knew Jonah needed to get help, and this was one time Jonah didn't care if the spirited horse wanted to run, because he had to get home as soon as he could!

"Did Jonah say what time he'd be home?" Sarah asked her husband, Raymond, as they sat down at the kitchen table for lunch.

Raymond shrugged his shoulders. "Just said he was going fishin', so guess it all depends on how well things go. I'm sure he'll be home before supper, though."

They bowed their heads for silent prayer, and then Sarah passed Raymond the potato salad she'd made. "Sadie Stoltzfus came by here this morning. Said she wanted to speak with Jonah."

"Oh, really? What about?"

"I don't know. Whatever it was, it must have been serious, because she looked quite agitated." Sarah took a tuna sandwich then handed the plate to Raymond. "You don't suppose it had anything to do with Meredith, do you?"

He reached for a sandwich and took a bite. "Beats me. What makes you think that, anyways?" he asked.

"Well, our son has been helping Meredith quite a bit lately, and since Meredith's husband was Sadie's son, she might not like it."

"Why would she care who helps Meredith?"

"She might be worried that Jonah has a personal interest in Meredith." Sadie took a few potato chips from the bowl in front of her then passed it on to Raymond.

"Would that be so terrible?" he questioned, his eyebrows lifting slightly.

"I don't think so, but Sadie might. She may not have come to terms with Luke's death yet. The idea of Jonah or any other man taking her son's place in Meredith's life might be too painful for her."

Raymond rubbed the bridge of his nose, looking at her with a thoughtful expression. "I suppose you might be right about that. Even so, it's Meredith's life, not Sadie's or anyone else's, so she ought to be free to begin her life again with the man of her choice, when the time is right."

Sarah nodded. "I totally agree."

Just then, the back door swung open, and Jonah, soaking wet and dripping water all over the floor, hobbled into the kitchen, wearing only one boot.

"What happened to you?" Sarah gasped, jumping out of her chair.

"A tree fell into the stream, and I got my left foot caught in its roots." Jonah grabbed the back of a chair for support and groaned. "My ankle's really swollen, and I either broke it or sprained it badly."

"You'd best get out of those wet clothes," Sarah said, heading to get the clothes basket. "And while you're daed's helping you with that, I'll go out to the phone shack and call the doctor—the one in the area who makes house calls to the Amish." She paused at the back door and pointed to a spot on Jonah's chest where his shirt hung open. "Ach, Jonah! Is that a leech?"

CHAPTER 6

"I don't like being laid up like this and unable to help with things," Jonah mumbled as he hobbled across the kitchen to the breakfast table. It had been two weeks since he'd broken his ankle, and even though he wore a walking cast, he couldn't do many things. Helping Dad paint the barn was out of the question right now. And he hadn't been able to go over to Meredith's and help with any chores. He missed their visits and the good food they shared whenever he'd been invited to stay for a meal. He longed to see Meredith's pretty face and enjoy their conversation.

"Don't be so impatient, Son." Mom gave Jonah's arm a tender squeeze. "You just need to stay off that foot as much as you can and give your ankle a chance to heal."

Dad bobbed his head. "Your *mamm*'s right. I can either paint the barn later this summer or I'll ask someone else to help me get it done."

"Who are you gonna ask?" Jonah reached for a piece of toast and slathered it with Mom's tasty homemade strawberry jam.

Dad shrugged. "Don't know yet. Guess I could ask my friend Harvey if his sons, Mahlon and Amos, might be available to help."

Jonah shook his head while he used his finger to wipe up some jam that had dripped onto his plate. "I think you should wait till I can help you." He paused to lick the jam from his finger and smacked his lips. "Those two boys probably don't know much about painting. They're farmers, Dad."

Dad took a drink of coffee. "Maybe you're

right. We can wait and paint the barn sometime in August."

"If you want to do it now, maybe I could sit on something and at least help to paint the bottom part of the barn," Jonah said. "I'd be off my feet, but I'd have something meaningful to do."

"I know how bad you want to help out around here, but it's probably best if you just keep resting that foot. There's nothin' critical that needs to be done, and the barn can wait a few more weeks," Dad assured him.

"Well, one thing I know for sure," Jonah said, reaching for his cup of coffee, "I'm going to sit on a stool and barbecue some steaks for supper this evening."

Mom grinned widely. "That sounds *wunderbaar*, Jonah. I'll make cucumber and pasta salads to go with the meat. There's nothing like nice cold salads for a meal during the hot summer months."

"And for dessert, I'll make a batch of homemade ice cream," Dad put in. "Is there any particular flavor you'd like?" he asked, looking at Jonah.

"Anything but orange," Jonah said, shaking his head. "Don't think I could tolerate that."

Mom chuckled. "You've always had an aversion to orange. Even when you were a boppli and I tried giving you orange juice, you'd make a face and spit the juice right out."

Dad chuckled. "I remember once when you and Jean were toddlers, you snitched her little pink sippy-cup, probably thinking it had milk it in, and boy, did you get a surprise when you took a drink."

"It wasn't so funny when he spit the juice all over Jean's new dress, and we ended up being late for church because I had to take the time out to change her clothes." Mom looked at Jonah and wrinkled her nose. "After that, you smelled everything you ate and drank to be sure it wasn't flavored with orange."

Jonah chuckled, despite his melancholy mood. It felt good to be living here in Pennsylvania with his folks, where they could enjoy being together and reminisce about the past. But he still wished he hadn't injured his ankle so he could do more to help them.

Meredith, too, he thought once again. *I can't wait till I'm able to pay her another visit and offer to do some needed chores.*

❦

"I'm sorry Jonah Miller broke his ankle," Sadie said to Elam as he sat at the table, reading the latest issue of *The Connection* magazine, while she cleared the breakfast dishes. "One good thing came out of it, though."

He looked up. "And what would that be?"

"Jonah's not going over to see Meredith right now."

"No, and you've made sure that we checked on her often, so that ought to make you happy."

Sadie poured Elam a second cup of coffee. "I'm always happy to see Meredith, but are you trying to make some particular point?"

He placed the magazine on the table and looked directly at her. "I just think you're overly *bekimmere* about Meredith."

"I have every right to be concerned. She's our daughter-in-law, for goodness' sake."

"That's true, but she's not our flesh and blood *dechder*, and as hard as this is to say, she's not married to our son any longer." Elam leveled Sadie with a stern look. "I think it's time you realize that Meredith has her own life to live, and you're not in control of her destiny."

Sadie recoiled. "I'm not trying to control her destiny. I just think Jonah, who isn't even part of the family, should not be doing things for her that we, as well as Meredith's family, ought to be doing."

"It's not our place to decide who should or shouldn't help Meredith. We should be grateful that not all the burden falls on just one person and that Jonah's willing to help her out."

Sadie set the coffeepot down and thumped the table. "You might think otherwise if Meredith ends up marrying Jonah."

Elam turned his hands palms-up. "If she does, she does. That will be her choice, not ours."

"So are you saying that you'd be okay with it if Meredith should marry Jonah?"

Elam gave a quick nod; then he pushed his chair away from the table, grabbed his straw hat from the wall peg across the room, and headed out the door.

Tears welled in Sadie's eyes. *I just can't bear the thought of Meredith becoming the wife of another man. Oh, I hope it doesn't come to that.*

❧

"It sure is a hot, humid day," Meredith commented to Laurie as they sat on the porch, drinking iced tea with lemon. They'd just gotten home from her eighth and final childbirth class. All the other sessions had been easy to get through: learning the breathing exercises and discovering each month how big the baby was as it grew inside of her; techniques for coping with pain; and how the partner could help during labor. This final class was the most intense and explained the birth in detail. Meredith didn't want to let on, but it made her a bit nervous to think about the pain she would experience and how long her labor might last. She knew that some women, like her friend Dorine, experienced a long labor with their first child.

I won't dwell on it, Meredith told herself. *I'll just wait and see how it all goes.*

She raised the drink to her face, enjoying the cool moisture of the glass as it touched her flushed cheek. "Thank goodness it was air-conditioned at the midwife's clinic," she said to her sister.

"That's for sure." Laurie lifted her dark apron and fanned her face with the edge of it. "It's times like this when I wish we had air-conditioning like Kevin has in his car."

"Speaking of Kevin, have Dad and Mom said anything more about you going out with him?"

Laurie nodded. "I think they've finally accepted it, but I know they were hoping I'd fall in love with an Amish man and join the church." She sighed. "Since Kevin and his parents attend a more modern Mennonite church and don't use horses and buggies for transportation, Mom and Dad are concerned that I'll succumb to worldly ways."

"Has Kevin considered joining the Amish church?" Meredith questioned.

"No. If he did that, he wouldn't be able to

drive his car anymore, and I'm sure he'd have a hard time giving that up."

"But if he loves you enough, he should be willing to give up anything." Meredith's thoughts went quickly to Luke. He'd owned a car during his running-around years but had gladly given it up when it was time to join the church and later get married.

"It's not just his car he'd have to give up," Laurie said. "Kevin wants to become a missionary, and I want that, too. I think it'd be a real adventure, not to mention an opportunity to help others and tell them about the Lord."

Meredith's eyes widened. "You mean move away to some foreign country?"

Laurie nodded. "Kevin has gone on some work-and-witness trips with a group from his church, and he feels that mission work is what God's calling him to do."

"Do Mom and Dad know about this?" Meredith asked.

"Jah. I told them last evening when I stopped by the house to get some clean clothes before I came here to spend the night."

"What'd they say?"

"Mom was pretty upset, but Dad took it fairly well. Said I should pray about it—make sure I felt the same call on my life as Kevin does before I commit to marrying him."

Meredith nodded. "I think that was sound advice." She placed her hands against her ever-growing stomach and smiled. "I've already begun praying for my boppli's future—that he or she will make wise choices and someday find the right spouse."

"Your little one will be making an appearance sometime soon." Laurie reached over and placed her hand next to Meredith's. "Are you feeling *naerfich* about giving birth?"

"I'm a little nervous," Meredith admitted. "The childbirth classes we've taken have been a big help in preparing me for what to do and what to expect. And I must say, I'm glad this morning was the last session, because it means my time is getting close." She sighed deeply. "I just wish my boppli's daed could be here to witness the birth of our child."

The babe kicked, as if in response to

what Meredith had just said. "Feel this," she said, taking hold of Laurie's hand and placing it against her stomach. "I do believe my little one's as anxious to make his appearance as I am for him to get here."

Philadelphia

"It's a warm day, isn't it, Eddie?" Anne asked as the two of them sat on a bench on the hospital grounds.

He gave a slow nod. "But it feels good to be outside in the fresh air."

Anne smiled. "Since part of your therapy is getting you back on your feet, walking and spending time outdoors is a good thing."

Eddie glanced around and breathed in deeply. Humid as it was, the air smelled so refreshing—not like it was inside the facility. Oh, it was nice and comfortable in the rehab center, and so clean you could probably eat off the floors, but he didn't enjoy the medicinal odors in some parts of the hospital.

Outside where they sat, flowers and bushes were in full bloom, and a small pond a short distance away reflected the beauty of their surroundings. Eddie could see several goldfish swimming around in the shaded part of the pond, and he wished he could join them in the nice cool water. It would be better than sitting here doing nothing at all and knowing that he didn't have anything to look forward to when they went back inside. It was lonely in his room, and he felt frustrated seeing other patients in rehab receiving visits from family members. Eddie had no family to encourage him, but he was thankful for Anne and her sister, Susan, who continually offered their support. He enjoyed Susan's chatter when she came to visit, which wasn't often enough to suit him. Of course, Eddie realized that she kept busy with her nursing duties, but he wished she could come to see him every day. Anne was nice, too, but she didn't talk to him as much as Susan did, and she seemed a little older and more serious about life than her sister.

"See that birdhouse over there?" Anne said, pointing.

Eddie nodded.

"A pair of bluebirds raised their babies in it last summer, and I've been watching to see if they'd return to their little home again this year."

Eddie just kept staring at the fish. They really had no place to go, except around and around the circumference of the pond. *Kind of like me,* he thought regrettably. *I have nowhere to go but here.*

"Well, would you look at those two?" Anne giggled.

Eddie looked toward a big rock that was nestled in one of the flower beds. Two wrens in front of the rock were taking turns trying to snatch a scrap of food away from each other. It looked like they'd found a piece of bread crust, and it was too big for either one of the birds to fly away with it. One of the birds would steal it from the other and run a few feet away from the one competing. Then the other wren did the same, with neither of them wanting to give up the precious morsel they'd found. This rivalry between the two little birds went on for several minutes until the scrap of bread was small enough for one bird to fly away with it. Not far behind, was the other wren, flying close to its competitor's tail.

Eddie smiled, until another thought popped into his mind. "Who's gonna pay for all my hospital bills?" he asked, turning to look at Anne. "I have no money."

Anne placed her hand gently on his arm. "You don't need to worry about that, Eddie. The hospital will absorb your expenses, just like they do with others in your situation."

Eddie sat, trying to digest that piece of information. It didn't seem right for him not to pay. If he knew who he was, maybe there'd be a relative who'd be willing to help out with his expenses. If he could just remember something—anything at all, it would be better than the way things were right now. All he had was a big blank hole in his life that might never be filled with memories from the past. His future looked pretty bleak and frightening.

CHAPTER 7

Bird-in-Hand

It was the first Monday of July, and as Meredith took a seat in the hickory rocker on her front porch, she looked up at the gray clouds overhead and yawned. She'd had a hard time sleeping last night, and tonight would probably be the same, because the air was warm and thick with moisture. In this kind of weather, a person didn't have to do much of anything to break out in a sweat.

Alma was inside, taking a nap, and would be

here with Meredith until Laurie got home this evening. Meredith had gotten used to having either her sister or Alma staying with her. She appreciated their help, and it was nice to have someone other than Fritz to talk to. Eventually, though, that would come to an end. Laurie would no doubt marry Kevin, and Alma was getting up in years. Besides, Meredith wanted to be on her own once the baby came; although there would be some chores she'd still need help with.

Maybe Jonah will continue to help out once he gets his cast off, Meredith thought. Between Jonah, Dad, and Luke's father coming by to do the outside chores, Meredith was sure she could manage the inside things on her own.

She glanced at the garden, overflowing with produce. *I really should pick some tomatoes and cucumbers.* It would be nice to have them along with the fried chicken and pasta salad Alma said she would fix for supper.

Meredith bent to pick up the wicker basket on the porch and winced when a sharp pain shot through her back. She stood, drawing in a deep breath and releasing it slowly. It would be a relief when the baby came and she could do things easily again. Based on what she'd learned about the final weeks of pregnancy at the childbirth classes, it wouldn't be long now.

When the pain subsided, Meredith headed for the garden. She was tempted to get on her knees to pick the beans but was afraid she might not be able get back up on her own. Placing the basket on the ground, she leaned over the best she could and started picking.

Meredith had only pulled a few beans from the vine when her friend Dorine Yoder rode in on her scooter.

"Wie geht's?" Dorine asked, parking the scooter near the porch.

"I'm doing okay," Meredith replied, making no mention of her painful back. There was no point in complaining about it. "What brings you by on this hot afternoon, and where are your *kinner?*"

"Merle and Cathy are with my mamm." Dorine smiled. "And since the children are well occupied, I decided to come over here and see how you're doing."

"I'd be better if this weather would cool down some," Meredith said. "Even standing still makes me sweat."

Dorine wiped the perspiration from her forehead. "I know what you mean. Unfortunately, we still have over two months until fall's officially here, and we could have hot, humid weather even into September."

"I know." Meredith blew out a puff of air. "The heat probably won't bother me so much once the boppli is born. All this heat is beginning to get to me, though. I think the dog days of summer are definitely upon us."

"Which is why you shouldn't be out here in the hot sun." Dorine picked up the basket of beans and motioned to the porch. "Now go sit and rest while I finish picking these for you."

Meredith didn't argue. She was more than ready to return to her seat on the porch. "Danki for being willing to help," she said, giving Dorine a hug.

Dorine gently patted Meredith's back. "That's what friends are for, you know."

As Meredith made her way back to the

porch, she thanked God for the wonderful friendship she and Dorine shared. They'd been close for several years, and Meredith had always enjoyed Dorine's easygoing ways and pleasant company.

Philadelphia

"How'd things go with Eddie today?" Susan asked her sister as they rode home from the hospital that afternoon.

"He's progressing," Anne replied. "What he seems to enjoy most is the therapy walks outside, getting fresh air, and especially sitting at the nature gardens. I think sometime within the next few weeks he might be strong enough to be seen as an outpatient. Of course, that will be up to his attending physician."

Susan felt immediate concern. "Where will Eddie go? He doesn't have a house, a job, or any family to go home to. The poor man doesn't even know who he is."

"You've formed an attachment to him, haven't you?" Anne asked, glancing over at Susan.

"I'm concerned, if that's what you mean."

"I think it goes deeper than that." Anne tapped the steering wheel a couple of times. "I believe you've formed an emotional attachment to Eddie."

Susan sat a few seconds; then she finally nodded. "Okay, yeah; I guess maybe I have. He seems like a really nice person, and it saddens me to think he may never know who his family is or be able to contact them. It's hard not being able to be there for him as much as I'd like to."

"I understand. It saddens me as well that he's in such a predicament." Anne turned her blinker on to change lanes. "What would you think about us asking Grandpa and Grandma if they'd be willing to take Eddie into their home in exchange for him doing some work around the place?"

"Are you kidding me? That would be great, if they're willing. But how would Eddie get to and from the hospital for his therapy sessions?" Susan questioned.

"If any of the sessions should fall on your day off, maybe you could take him to the hospital, or we could see if Grandpa would be willing."

Susan smiled. "I like that idea, and if I know Grandma and Grandpa, they'll be happy to take Eddie in. I can already imagine Grandma's eagerness. You know how she is. The more people she can cook for, the better she likes it."

"Great. We can talk to them about it as soon as we get home."

❧

Darby

Norma Bailey hummed as she sliced a hefty beefsteak tomato for the BLTs they would have for supper. It was a warm summer evening— too hot to heat up the kitchen with the oven. Anne and Susan would be getting home from work soon, and then they'd eat outside under the shade of the maple tree while they visited about their day and made plans for the weekend.

Norma had talked to her friend, Mary

Hagen, today, and she was looking forward to following through on the invitation they'd been given to visit the Hagens' home for a meal after church this coming Sunday. The best part was that Mary and Ben's grandson Brian would be there. Norma had been hoping Susan would get the chance to meet Brian while he was visiting his grandparents this summer, and this looked like the perfect opportunity.

She smiled and set the plate of tomatoes aside. If the young couple should hit it off, maybe Brian would decide to stay in the area permanently. *And maybe,* Norma thought, feeling hope well in her chest, *at least one of our granddaughters will get married and give Henry and me some great-grandchildren.*

"Is there anything I can do to help you, Norma?" Henry asked when he entered the kitchen a few minutes later. "I got the picnic table wiped off, so that much is done." He chuckled. "And you should have heard George out there, chattering away at me. I think he knows we'll be eating outside this evening."

George was a squirrel that for the last

couple of years had become almost tame around Norma and Henry. They'd noticed how every time they were in the backyard working or eating at the picnic table, this curious little squirrel would appear and patiently sit and watch until they went back inside. Norma and Henry had started talking to the squirrel and tried not to pose a threat to it. Of course, it helped that Henry always had some sort of a snack in his pocket that he used, hoping to entice the little gray critter each time he went outside. One day the squirrel walked right up to Henry and took the morsel gently out of his hand. From that time on, little George became their outdoor pet.

"Yes, I'm sure George will be waiting nearby for a handout," Norma said, smiling. Then she motioned to the toaster. "If you'd like to toast the bread for the sandwiches, I'll start frying the bacon. Oh, would you also open that new loaf of bread? There's only a few slices left in the other package, and we'll share those with George."

"Sure, I can do that." Henry reached around

Norma, snatched a tomato slice, and popped it into his mouth. "Mmm. . .my garden has been producing some delicious tomatoes this year, don't ya think? Look how meaty these are," he said, pausing to wipe the juice dripping down his chin. "And there are hardly any seeds in them, either."

She nodded. "But if you keep eating the tomato slices, I'll have to cut up some more."

He chuckled. "That's okay. There's plenty more where these babies came from."

"I know that." Norma paused, using a napkin to dab at the spot where some tomato juice had dribbled onto her husband's shirt. "I'd just like to have everything ready when the girls get home."

"What else are we having besides BLTs?" he asked.

"I made a macaroni salad and added some shrimp and a little crabmeat."

He smacked his lips. "Always did like a good seafood salad."

As Henry took care of toasting the bread and Norma fried the bacon, they discussed the garden, the weather, and their friends from church.

"I sure hope Susan and Anne will join us at the Hagens' for dinner on Sunday," Norma said, turning off the stove after the bacon was nice and crispy.

"I'm sure they will if they haven't made other plans," Henry said.

Sponging up some of the bacon grease that had splattered on the stove, Norma was about to bring up the topic of Susan meeting Brian, but she changed her mind. Henry would probably accuse her of trying to play matchmaker again, and she didn't want any lectures from him. She'd just have to wait and see how things went. She'd like nothing more than to see her granddaughters find someone special to spend the rest of their lives with. Norma knew, deep down, that it wasn't up to her, but she couldn't help hoping Susan and Anne would one day have a wonderful marriage like she and Henry had. *Well,* Norma reasoned, *it doesn't hurt for me to hope.*

Anne and Susan arrived home just as Norma finished putting the sandwiches together. "Oh, good, you're right on time, because supper's ready," Norma said, turning to smile at her granddaughters. "And we're going to eat our meal in the backyard this evening."

Susan grinned. "That's good, 'cause I'm more than ready to eat."

"Me, too," Anne agreed as she and Susan washed up at the kitchen sink. "I'm really glad we're eating outside. After being cooped up in rehab all day, I'm in need of some fresh air and sunshine. The only time I get to go outside is during my short breaks or when I'm walking with Eddie for his therapy."

"Well, let's get started then," Norma said. "If you two would like to carry the macaroni salad and pitcher of lemonade out to the picnic table, I'll bring the tray with paper plates, silverware, and sandwiches."

"I'll grab a bag of chips and the pieces of bread for little George," Henry said, winking at the girls.

When they were all seated around the picnic table, Henry led in prayer. "Dear heavenly Father," he said, "we thank You for the delicious meal set before us and for the hands that prepared it. We also want to give thanks for the beautiful warm weather we've had so far this summer, and for the many blessings You've bestowed upon us. Amen." He opened his eyes and smiled. Grabbing a sandwich, he announced with a twinkle in his eyes, "Let's dig in!"

As they ate in their pleasant backyard, a chorus of birds sang overhead, and several butterflies flitted from one flower to another. The conversation was mostly centered around Anne and Susan, and how things had gone for them at the hospital that day.

"It was even busier than usual in ICU," Susan said. "A couple of new patients were brought in this morning, and we were shorthanded besides, with one nurse out sick and another on vacation."

"Things were pretty crazy in rehab, too," Anne interjected.

"How's that Eddie fellow doing?" Henry asked.

"He's making some headway with every-thing except his memory," Anne replied, before taking a drink of lemonade.

"Speaking of Eddie," Susan quickly said, "if he keeps progressing, he should be well enough to be released from the hospital in a few weeks. Only trouble is, he has no place to go, so he'll probably have to stay on, like so many other patients do when they have no home or family."

Henry slowly shook his head. "I read an article awhile back about that very thing. Guess the hospitals can't simply throw someone out in the street when they're well and have no place to go. So they often keep them there until some other arrangements can be made. Of course, that means the hospital must absorb the cost of the patient's care."

"That's too bad," Norma said. "It's a shame to think about all the people right here in our state who are homeless."

"Susan and I were talking about Eddie on the way home." Anne looked first at Henry and then Norma. "We were wondering if you two might consider letting him stay here in exchange for whatever work you might want to have done."

Henry sat, rubbing his chin, but it wasn't long before Norma tapped his arm and said, "I think that's an excellent idea. Maybe Eddie can help you paint the outside of the house."

"I don't think he should do anything too strenuous," Anne was quick to say. "At least not until he's a bit stronger."

"Oh, you're right, of course. Maybe at first he could just do some light chores—or help with some yard work." Norma nudged Henry's arm again. "What do you think? Should we let Eddie stay with us—at least until he gets his memory back and is able to move out on his own?"

Henry sat quietly for several more seconds then finally nodded. "If it doesn't work out, though, we'll have to find him a place at the homeless shelter."

CHAPTER 8

Bird-in-Hand

$\mathcal{M}$eredith shifted on the backless wooden bench where she'd taken a seat almost three hours ago in Deacon Raber's barn. Her back hurt something awful, and no matter how hard she tried, she couldn't seem to find a comfortable position. She glanced over at Laurie, sitting straight on the bench beside her, with her hands clasped in her lap. She didn't look uncomfortable at all.

I wonder how many more times I'll get to sit beside

my sister like this in church? Meredith wondered. *If Laurie marries Kevin Byler and they move to some foreign country, I may never see her again.*

A cramping sensation gripped Meredith's stomach, causing her thoughts to redirect. *Maybe I should have stayed home from church this morning.* Due to the back pain and a few stomach cramps that had finally gone away last night, she hadn't slept well. She'd had another dream about Luke, too, which had woken her around four o'clock this morning. It was hard to believe he'd been gone nearly six months already, yet there were times when it seemed like only yesterday that they'd said their goodbyes on the porch.

Will the pain of losing Luke lessen or increase after the boppli is born? Meredith asked herself as she reached around and placed her hands on the lower part of her back. One thing for sure: she'd be glad when the baby arrived, for the heat and humidity of summer was really getting to her. That, coupled with her top-heavy stomach and inability to do many things, made her feel cross at times.

When Mom had dropped by for a visit the

other day, she had told Meredith that she'd felt irritable and unproductive with each of her pregnancies that had occurred during the heat of summer. While Mom was there, she'd also lectured Meredith on the importance of getting plenty of rest and staying hydrated. Meredith was drinking lots of water, but it was hard to rest when she felt so miserable and couldn't find a comfortable position. If this unrelenting backache didn't ease by evening, she might have to consider sleeping in one of the recliners in her living room.

Meredith shifted on the bench once more and glanced across the room to where the men and boys sat. She spotted Jonah and noticed that he seemed to be staring at her. Hoping no one else had seen, she gave him a brief nod then quickly looked away. It was one thing for Jonah to drop by her house on occasion, to do a few chores, but she didn't want anyone here to get the idea that she might be interested in him.

Am I interested? she asked herself. *If Jonah were to ask me to marry him after my year of mourning is up, what would I say? I enjoy his company, and I'm sure he'd be a good daed to my boppli, but is that enough? Could I ever feel the kind of love in my heart for Jonah that I've felt for Luke ever since we first became serious about each other and got engaged? Down the road things might change, but right now, I'm thinking probably not.*

When their church service concluded, Jonah was tempted to seek Meredith out but thought better of it. From the way she looked during the service, she didn't feel very well. She appeared to be tired and seemed fidgety, like she couldn't find a comfortable position on the bench. A couple of times he'd noticed Meredith placing her hands against her lower back, as if to support it. He could only imagine how uncomfortable that hard wooden bench must be for a woman so far along in her pregnancy—especially sitting there for three whole hours.

If he saw a chance to speak to her when nobody else was around, he would take it. Otherwise, to avoid scrutiny, visiting with Meredith would have to wait until he could stop by her house again. It didn't help that he still had his foot in the immobility boot and couldn't do much to help with any chores, but he would be getting the boot off soon and would be glad to get back to doing things again.

Jonah was thankful he'd been blessed with loving, understanding parents. Not everyone, Amish or English, could say the same.

After the noon meal, Jonah noticed Meredith and her sister head for their buggy. They were obviously going home, and he resigned himself to the fact that he wouldn't get the chance to speak with her today.

Sure wish it was me taking Meredith home instead of Laurie, he thought ruefully. *I wonder if I'll ever be able to tell Meredith how I feel about her. If I did, what would she say?*

❧

Philadelphia

As Susan headed down the hall toward Eddie's room in the rehab wing of the hospital, she thought about everything the poor man had been through over the past six months. From what Anne had told her, Eddie worked hard in therapy, consistently striving to improve his physical abilities. She credited his progress to a positive attitude and persistence, whereas many patients would have given up by now.

Anxious to talk with Eddie on her day off about the possibility of moving to Grandma and Grandpa's, she'd decided to visit right after church. Besides, she'd learned that Brian, the Hagens' grandson, would be at lunch this afternoon, which made her suspect that Grandma was up to her old matchmaking tricks.

Susan wasn't having any of that, so as soon as the service had ended, she'd told Grandma that she was going to the hospital to see Eddie. She could tell by Grandma's frown that she wasn't happy about it, but at least she hadn't put up a fuss. Maybe she'd changed her strategy and had decided that Anne and Brian would make a better match, because she seemed quite happy when Anne said she'd be pleased to join them at the Hagens' house for lunch. Either way, Susan was glad she'd had an excuse to duck out.

When Susan got to Eddie's room, he wasn't there. She checked at the nurses' station and was told that Eddie had taken a walk. Thinking he might be in the garden area outside, Susan headed in that direction.

When she stepped into the courtyard, she spotted Eddie sitting on a bench, with a fluffy white kitten in his lap. He looked like a cute little boy, content and relaxed as he gently stroked the kitten's head.

"I see you've made a new friend," Susan said, taking a seat beside Eddie.

His beautiful turquoise eyes sparkled as he grinned. "I heard some meowing in the bushes, and when I went to take a look, she leaped right out and started pawing at my leg, like she wanted me to pick her up. So I did."

Susan smiled. It was refreshing to meet a man with such a tender spirit. She wondered if he'd ever had any pets of his own. If he had, he'd probably treated them with the same gentleness he was using on this kitten right now, as it purred and rubbed its small head against Eddie's hand. The kitten was definitely content lying there in his lap.

They visited about the warm, sticky weather; then Eddie told Susan about his latest physical therapy session in a jetted spa tub. He mentioned that he enjoyed being in the water and felt like he was getting stronger every day.

"I'm glad. I know it's taken a long time and lots of patience, but it's been worth the effort, don't you think?"

He nodded. "I'm hoping that as my body becomes stronger my brain will heal, as well. If I could just figure out who I am, I could leave this hospital soon."

"Has Anne said anything to you about moving to our grandparents' home?" Susan asked.

"Yes, she did, and I'm glad they're agreeable, but now that I've had some time to think about it, I'm not sure it's such a good idea."

"How come?"

"For one thing, I have no money and wouldn't be able to pay them any room and board."

"You'll earn your keep by helping out with some chores."

"But why would they want to take a total stranger into their home? For all they know, I might be a terrible person."

"Do you think you're a terrible person, Eddie?" Susan questioned.

He shook his head. "I don't feel like I am, but since I can't remember anything about my past, guess I could have done some terrible things."

"I doubt it," she said, reaching over to stroke the kitten's head. "You're kind and gentle, even with this little stray kitten, so I'm thinking you've always been like that."

Eddie sat quietly for several minutes, then he released a soft moan.

"What's wrong? Are you in pain?" she asked, feeling concern.

"Not here," he said, touching his head. "But here." He placed his hand over his heart. "I've been having nightmares lately where I see a woman holding her arms out to me, but she has no face." He looked at Susan, and his beautiful turquoise eyes seemed to penetrate her soul. "I know it wasn't you I was dreaming about, 'cause if it had been, I'm sure I'd have seen your pretty face."

A rush of heat spread over Susan's cheeks. Was Eddie flirting with her? Did she want him to? "Thanks for the compliment," she murmured. Knowing she needed to get back to the subject of where he would stay, she quickly said, "You know, Eddie, if you take a room at my grandparents' place, we'll see each other more, because Anne and I live there, too."

Eddie's face brightened. "You do?"

She nodded. "We've been with Grandma and Grandpa ever since our folks were killed in a car crash when we were girls."

Deep wrinkles formed across his forehead. "I'm sorry to hear about your folks, but I think your grandpa and grandma must have done a good job raising you 'cause you and your sister are the nicest women I've ever known." He dropped his gaze, and his shoulders slumped. "Course, I'm not sure how many women I've known before."

She gave his shoulder a gentle squeeze. "So, how about it, Eddie? Are you willing to stay at my grandparents' house when the doctor releases you as an outpatient?"

He nodded slowly, while stroking the kitten's head. "If your grandparents are anything like you and Anne, then I'm sure I'll like it there."

Bird-in-Hand

"Are you okay?" Laurie asked Meredith as they rode in the buggy toward Meredith's home. "You look downright miserable today."

"My back hurts really bad, and I've been having twinges all morning." Meredith touched her stomach. "I'll sure be glad when the boppli is born."

Laurie's eyes widened as she turned to look at Meredith. "You're not in labor, I hope."

Meredith shook her head and flinched when the buggy hit a bump in the road. "At least, I don't think I am."

"How bad is the pain? Should we turn around and head back so you can talk to Mom about this?"

"No, I don't think it's anything to worry about. I'm not due for a couple more weeks, and most first-time mothers that I know have been late, not early, giving birth."

"But everyone's different," Laurie said, clucking to the horse to get him moving faster. "Remember what they said at the last childbirth class? Those back pains you're having could be labor pains, after all."

"I suppose, but—" Meredith grimaced. "Oh, oh."

"What's wrong Meredith?" Laurie's voice held a note of panic.

"My water just broke, and. . ." Meredith winced. "I—I think the boppli wants to be born today, not two weeks from now."

"Hang on while I look for the nearest phone shack so I can call for help."

Another pain came, this one harder than the last. "You'd better pull over, Laurie. I can't believe it, but it's happening so fast." Meredith clenched her fingers until they dug into her palms. "I think I may have been in labor during the night and didn't even realize it."

"Well, you can't have the boppli until we get you some help, 'cause I can't help you birth the baby." Laurie's voice shook, and so did her hands.

"Jah, you can," Meredith said, working to keep her own voice calm. She tried to think of that verse of scripture she'd memorized awhile back. It was something about God giving peace, and not being afraid.

Oh, yes, now I remember. John 14:27. "Peace I leave with you, my peace I give unto you: not as the world giveth, give I unto you. Let not your heart be troubled, neither let it be afraid." If she kept her focus on that, she wouldn't feel so frightened.

She turned to Laurie and quoted the verse aloud. Then she said, "You've gone with me to all the birthing classes, and the last one we attended was all about the birth, so you know what to do. Just try not to be afraid." She took her sister's hand and gave it a squeeze.

"We can get through this together."

Laurie shook her head vigorously, as though she hadn't heard a word Meredith said. "No, I don't want to do it, Meredith. I'm terribly frightened I'll do something to mess up. All I know is how to help you through the birthing process by reminding you how to breathe and coaching you along. I can't deliver the boppli, Meredith. I'd be too naerfich."

Another pain came, harder than the last, and Meredith shouted, "Pull over, Laurie— right now!" Breathing deeply, she held on to the edge of her seat. "This boppli is coming, whether you like it or not!"

ABOUT THE AUTHOR

New York Times bestselling author Wanda E. Brunstetter became fascinated with the Amish way of life when she first visited her husband's Mennonite relatives living in Pennsylvania. Wanda and her husband, Richard, live in Washington State but take every opportunity to visit Amish settlements throughout the States, where they have several Amish friends. Wanda and her husband have two grown children and six grandchildren. In her spare time, Wanda enjoys photography, ventriloquism, gardening, beachcombing, stamping, and having fun with her family.

Visit Wanda's website at www.wandabrunstetter.com.

Join Wanda on Facebook!

If you're a fan of Amish Fiction, you'll "Like" Wanda's official Facebook page!

"Like" Wanda's page and you'll...

· See announcements of upcoming releases
· Participate in contests
· View video trailers
· Find out if Wanda is going to be in your area
· Learn more about Amish life
· Connect with other fans of Amish Fiction

This is the best place to keep up
on Wanda's news, books, and travels.
Search for Wanda E. Brunstetter on www.facebook.com